the List

KEITH GRAY

Barrington  Stoke

Published by Barrington Stoke
An imprint of HarperCollins*Publishers*
Westerhill Road, Bishopbriggs, Glasgow, G64 2QT

www.barringtonstoke.co.uk

HarperCollins*Publishers*
Macken House, 39/40 Mayor Street Upper,
Dublin 1, DO1 C9W8, Ireland

First published in 2024

Text © 2024 Keith Gray
Cover illustration © 2024 Tom Clohosy Cole
Cover design © 2024 HarperCollins*Publishers* Limited

The moral right of Keith Gray to be identified
as the author of this work has been asserted in accordance
with the Copyright, Designs and Patents Act, 1988

ISBN 978-1-80090-320-3

10 9 8 7 6 5 4 3 2 1

A catalogue record for this book is available from the British Library

Printed and bound in India by Replika Press Pvt. Ltd.

MIX
Paper | Supporting
responsible forestry
FSC™ C007454

This book contains FSC™ certified paper and other controlled
sources to ensure responsible forest management.

For more information visit: www.harpercollins.co.uk/green

For Lucy

*(and there's a long list
of reasons why ...)*

5 DAYS TO GO

CHAPTER 1

We had less than a week of the summer holidays left. Me and Denny were sitting on his bedroom floor staring at the empty cardboard box in between us. Denny rubbed his eyes with the back of his fists.

"It's hay fever that's making my eyes itch," Denny lied. I could tell he was trying not to cry. His deep brown eyes were as shiny as snooker balls.

August was almost over. Denny's bedroom window was wide open, letting in the last of the summer's warmth. He leaned back against the wall, hugged his legs to his chest and buried his face between his knees. He sniffed hard but still left a damp trail of snot on one knee of his jeans.

Denny had always been shorter and skinnier than me but his unhappiness seemed to shrink him even more today. It curled him up tight.

Earlier that morning, Denny's mum had told him he needed to start packing. There was a stack of flat cardboard boxes in the middle of the carpet between us. They all needed to be made up but in the past hour Denny had only put together one box. There were at least another twelve boxes in the stack.

Denny and his mum were moving away on Sunday. In five days' time my best friend would be going to live miles away in a place I'd never even heard of.

I knew Denny had been putting off thinking about moving. I knew I'd been pretending it wasn't going to happen too.

We stared at the empty box but didn't talk. Sitting in silence began to feel too awkward, so I stood up and started to move about.

The bedroom walls were covered in Denny's drawings. It must have cost him a fortune in Blu-Tack to stick them all up. Most of the pictures were stuff he'd copied from comics but he was also getting good at drawing stuff from around the village too. He'd even drawn himself sitting on a horse called Burdock from a few years ago.

"It's going to take ages to pack all your drawings," I said.

Denny just shrugged.

I looked at the delicate dead wasps' nest on the bookshelf and wondered how Denny was going to box it up without crushing it. He had a collection of amazing and colourful shells on his windowsill. And a Venus flytrap he called "Dave". In the corner on the floor were two towering piles of read and re-read comics. I couldn't help worrying that some of Denny's favourite things might get damaged in the move.

I looked out of the open bedroom window and over Denny's back garden to the golf course beyond. Denny's house was on a small lane right at the edge of the village and the houses here backed onto Pensing Hill Golf Course. Our parents weren't members of the local golf club, so the course was strictly out of bounds to us. We sometimes found stray golf balls in his garden and always kept them. Finders keepers. I preferred the coloured balls to the boring white ones.

I could see golfers strolling across the sunny green grass in the distance. Denny said he hated golf, so I supposed I did too.

I heard Denny groan. "I can't be arsed with this," he grunted. He lashed out with his foot and kicked the stack of flat boxes, spilling them across the floor. "Come on," he told me, jumping up.

"Where are we going?" I asked.

Denny stamped down on the one box he'd made, smashing it flat again. "Let's just go," he said.

I followed Denny downstairs, happy to get out of his bedroom. I normally felt as comfortable in his room as I did in my own. But in five days' time it would suddenly become somebody else's room. A total stranger would fill it with all their favourite things, and that was such a weird thought. Weird and a little bit scary.

Denny slammed the front door behind us as we left the house. He kicked open his garden gate, banging it back on its squeaky metal hinges. He kicked the gate closed again, making it shudder and clang. In the quiet lane, all that noise felt shocking.

We walked side by side along the pavement. Denny and Jake. Jake and Denny. It had been that way for as long as we could remember. We were different but kind of the same. I was taller and Denny was skinnier with longer, messier and darker hair. But our T-shirts, jeans and trainers almost matched – except that morning I didn't have dried snot on one knee.

Denny pointed at his next-door neighbours' neat and tidy house. "I bet they don't care I'm leaving," he said. Then he pointed at the house with the big tree in the garden on the other side of the lane. "I reckon they're going to have a party to celebrate when I go."

He strode out into the middle of the road, pointing at another house, and another, and another. "And them. And them. And them," he said. "I bet you no one cares."

I hoped he knew that I cared. School started again next week and I was struggling to get my head around the idea that I'd be going into Year 9 alone.

"It's not fair," Denny groaned.

"What's not fair?" I asked. "That the people who live here don't care about you leaving?"

"Stuff them," Denny shouted. He waved his hands in the air with his middle fingers pointing at the sky. "I don't care about any of them."

"So it's not fair that you've got to move?" I asked.

"It's not fair that I've got to move *now*," he said. "I'm not ready."

"Because you've not packed yet?" I asked.

"I'm not ready because there's still loads I want to do," he replied.

I was confused. "Like what?"

Denny surprised me by spinning round on the spot and stomping off back the way we'd come. I had to run to catch up as he banged and clanged through his garden gate again. He went round the side of his house past the garage. I asked him what he was doing but he didn't answer.

The back garden was a messy, colourful jungle because Denny's mum loved flowers but never had much time for mowing or pruning or whatever. She worked two jobs, so it wasn't surprising. She loved her roses most of all and used manure from the local farmer to feed them.

On hot days like today you could sometimes catch a faint whiff of it.

The wooden fence at the bottom of the garden was tall but wobbly. Pensing Hill Golf Course was on the other side. Denny's mum must have told us a thousand times that we were totally, absolutely, one hundred per cent forbidden from ever climbing over.

So I was pretty shocked when Denny stood in between his mum's sprawling roses and jumped up to grab the top of the wobbly fence. He huffed and puffed as he pulled himself higher and scrambled his feet against the wood. He got his belly over the top, then sort of flopped, sort of fell down the other side.

"Denny?" I called. "Your mum will kill you if she finds out what you're doing."

Denny just shouted, "You coming or what?"

CHAPTER 2

Of course I followed Denny over the fence, despite knowing we could get into massive trouble for trespassing.

There was a bunker on the other side and I landed feet first in the sand. The bunker had high sides. We crouched down, staying hidden as we peered over the top at the wide, green golf course. It was a Tuesday morning, so there weren't many golfers out there. I counted only ten dotted around the course.

The two old men closest to where me and Denny were hidden were strolling slowly our way, chatting and dragging their golf bags on wheels. They hadn't spotted us clambering over the fence.

The golf course was so big it had its own mini hills and woods. The grass seemed somehow greener than the grass in the village park where we hung around most days. The park had a manky ducky pond but in the middle of the golf course there was a fake lake that was shaped like a kidney bean. The golf course was bigger than the park too, which could only fit half a footy pitch next to the kids' playground. The main entrance to the golf course with the car park and the clubhouse looked miles away from our bunker.

"What are we doing?" I asked Denny.

"I just wanted to be here," he said.

"OK," I said.

"I thought that, before I have to leave on Sunday, I wanted to be here. Because I've never been here before."

I understood. We weren't going to wreck anything or steal anything. We were just curious about this forbidden place that Denny could see out of his bedroom window.

"And what is anyone going to do if they catch me?" Denny went on. "I'm leaving anyway, right?"

"Right," I said. But I was also thinking that I wasn't leaving. If we got caught here, I'd have to face all of the grief and trouble myself. Not that I said that to Denny.

He pulled his phone out of the back pocket of his jeans. "Got to prove we were here, right?" he said.

We leaned back against the bunker's high sandy side with our heads poking over the top.

"Come on, Jake," Denny told me as we grinned smarmy grins for the selfie. "Say 'golf sucks'."

We both shouted it as he took the photo. And we both got sand down the backs of our necks.

Denny only used his phone to take photos. He'd begged and begged his mum for ages and ages to buy him a phone. Luckily for him, she'd finally caved in. But Denny never called or messaged anyone because his mum had said he would need to pay for his own contract after she'd bought the phone. He spent his money on comics instead.

Denny's phone was the exact same make and model as the one I used to have, except his had a silver-and-black cover. Mine had had a red-and-gold cover and I'd lost it back in December. My mum and dad had gone ballistic when I'd told them. I reckoned it had been stolen, so I'd tried to explain it wasn't totally my fault.

My parents had still refused to buy me another one. And being phone-less at thirteen is rubbish.

After taking the selfie, Denny and I had to duck down again fast because the two old men golfers were coming closer. One of them had very orange trousers, sunglasses and a white cap. His friend was bald with a beer belly that stretched his stripey shirt. They were heading towards the nearest hole and its green, which were only a few metres away from where me and Denny were hiding in the bunker.

"We're trapped," I whispered. The golfers would see us if we tried to get back over the fence into Denny's garden.

"We need a plan," Denny said. Then added, "Do you reckon we can make it to that bunker over there? See it?"

It was fifty, maybe sixty metres away and had tall bushes on one side.

"Maybe."

"Then that bunker, then that one," Denny went on, pointing further away towards the main entrance and clubhouse. "I bet we could run between bunkers all the way out."

We could hear the two old golfers talking. I dared to peer over the top of the bunker. The one in orange trousers pulled a club out of his trolley bag. He stood with his orange legs apart and did a couple of practice swings. Then he took a shot. We heard the *thwack*. His bald friend muttered, "Good shot."

But we didn't bother to see where his golf ball went. As soon as the old golfers had their backs to us, we were up and out of the bunker and sprinting across the grass. I checked behind me as we ran but the golfers hadn't spotted us. We dived head-first into the bushes and down into the second bunker. I got a mouthful of sand. Denny tumbled over, getting it in his curly hair.

Then we grinned great big grins at each other.

"Plan's working," Denny said. "Ready for the next one?"

I nodded. "Which way is it?"

This bunker wasn't as deep as the first one and we had to stay flat on our bellies. The sand was gritty and irritating. Denny rubbed at his curly hair.

"We go for that one on this side of the lake," Denny said. "It's further away but there's another golfer over near that other bunker, see?"

"You first," I said.

Denny's feet slipped a bit in the sand as he jumped up. Then we were both running over the soft grass again. Running fast but running quiet.

We were panting hard by the time we tumbled and skidded into the third bunker. We still hadn't been seen but we knew we couldn't hang around. We sprinted to a fourth bunker. Then a fifth, ducking low as we charged across the golf course. We dodged from view behind trees and bushes as we went.

We made it to the final bunker – the one closest to the car park and clubhouse. We had sand in our trainers and in our ears and stuck to the sweat on our faces. From here, there were no more bunkers to hide us. All we could do was stride out across the grass towards the main entrance, acting like we owned the place. Denny and Jake, pretending we were the sandy kings of the golf course. We knew the trick was not to act like we were guilty. A few people gave us surprised stares and confused frowns as we walked between the parked cars but we ignored them all.

We made it to the main gate underneath the huge Pensing Hill Golf Course sign and then started legging it again. Our feet pounded along the main road back towards the village. But we laughed out loud as we ran.

We were buzzing with what we'd done.

"That's number one," Denny said, puffing and panting between his laughter. "That was just the first thing I wanted to do before I have to leave on Sunday. I'm going to make a list of the other stuff. You'll help me, right?"

"Yeah, obviously," I said. "Of course." I spat out a mouthful of sand.

I hoped helping Denny would take my mind off counting down the days before he moved and I was left on my own.

4 DAYS LEFT ...

CHAPTER 3

The next day, Denny was waiting for me at the duck pond in the park. He had two black plastic buckets, one in each hand. Denny was excited, bubbly. I was tired, bleary-eyed. It was six in the morning. Even the ducks on the pond looked sleepy.

I only had one bucket. Mucky and brown. I'd found it at the back of Dad's shed, behind the lawnmower, and I'd had to tip out the spiders who'd been living inside.

"My mum wanted to know why I needed a bucket," I told Denny. I'd had to ask her last night if I could borrow it.

"What did you tell her?" he asked.

"I said that you wanted it. Because you had some kind of plan."

"And what did your mum say about that?" Denny asked.

"Nothing. She just rolled her eyes."

"I'll miss your mum," Denny said.

I nodded but stared down into my bucket at the tatty cobwebs still inside. Denny saying that about my mum gave me a sudden stab of sadness. My mum had already said she'd miss Denny too. Not as much as I would. But still.

Denny was always round my house, especially when his mum was working – which was a lot. He stayed for tea at ours two or three times a week and my mum was a bit stricter about him finishing his homework than his mum was. But Denny said that was a good thing.

I used to think it was cool that Denny had his own keys to his house and was free to roam without his mum being around all the time. At my house, if my mum wasn't there, then my dad was. Or my little brother, Mickey. I never got to spend time alone. Not that I wanted anyone to die! Denny's dad had died when he was only three and so it had been just him and his mum for a long time.

"What are the buckets really for?" I asked. I wanted to get on with it. Doing something was better than standing around thinking.

Denny stepped up to the edge of the pond and bent down to scoop water into one of his buckets. "We've got to fill them up," he said.

"Are you allowed to do that?" I asked. "Isn't it stealing?"

"Stealing pond water?" Denny scoffed.

I shrugged but still checked to see if we were being watched. Apart from a woman walking her dog by the footy pitch, we were alone in the park. She was talking on her phone while her dog chased a seagull which flapped up onto the crossbar of the goalposts. It was too early in the morning for any other kids to be hanging around.

I dunked my bucket into the pond and watched the murky water swirl inside. I caught a crisp packet and a clump of soggy duck feathers. I went to fish the crisp packet out but Denny stopped me. His buckets were so full the water sloshed over onto the path when he put them down. One of them had an empty vape pen floating in it.

"I've made that list I told you about," Denny said. He took a piece of paper out of his back pocket and as he unfolded it I saw it was covered in scribbles and crossings-out. "There's loads and loads I really want to do before I leave, so I've had to choose the most important."

The paper was almost all black scrawls except for five sentences that he'd underlined twice and circled in red.

Denny read the five sentences aloud. "One, get revenge on Mal. Two, re-live my first kiss. Three, say sorry to Mrs Hubler. Four, return what I stole. Five, ride Burdock again."

He read his list in a really serious tone of voice. He sounded like a boring vicar. Or like our head teacher had sounded during that special assembly last year when she'd told all the boys to stop peeing their names in the snow because it was disgusting and unhygienic.

"I don't get it," I said.

"What's to get?" Denny sounded offended.

"These are impossible, aren't they?" I said. It was my turn to go all serious. I pointed at his red-circled sentences one by one. "Mal's just gonna kick you in if you do anything to him.

There's no way on this planet you'll ever be able to get Tabby to kiss you again. Mrs Hubler probably wouldn't be happy even if you said sorry a hundred times. If you give back something you stole, then you'll have to admit you nicked it in the first place. And last time you tried to ride Burdock he bucked you off and you nearly broke your neck."

Denny scowled, angry with me. "So don't help me, then." He folded up his list.

"I never said I won't help, but ..." I shrugged.

"But what?" Denny asked.

I shrugged again.

"Look, I have to leave on Sunday," Denny said. "You're probably the only one who cares."

"My mum and dad care."

"Yeah, OK, maybe them. But no one else. And I swear, I really need to do this stuff." Denny waved his sheet of paper at me. "It's like I'm, you know, sort of tying up loose ends or something."

I felt like I began to understand. "Like setting the record straight?" I said.

"Exactly." Denny nodded.

"Leaving your mark?" I asked.

He nodded again and beamed his big grin. "That too."

"I still reckon they're impossible," I said.

Denny shoved his list back into his jeans pocket, swapping it for his phone. "I've got plans. And I want to remember *everything*." He took a photo of me standing there holding my bucket.

"So why did you make me get out of bed so early?" I asked. "And what are we meant to do with three buckets of pond water?"

"Top of the list," Denny said. "Getting revenge on Mal."

CHAPTER 4

Denny and I waddled out of the park onto the main road, struggling with our full buckets. The pond water slopped and splashed on the pavement. There was no one else around because it was still so early. Even the baker's wasn't open yet. It only took fifteen minutes to walk to Mal Bro's house. Nowhere in our village was much more than a fifteen-minute walk away. But the overflowing buckets were heavy, dragging on our arms and zapping our strength.

Our village was just a dot on the map but it felt bigger for those of us who lived there. The main road went from a "Check Your Speed" sign and the high school at one end to the "Thank You For Driving Carefully" sign and the golf course at the other. Beyond them were fields and farms. There was a handful of shops, the post office and a pub clumped together on the main road. The park, war memorial and church were opposite. Almost everybody knew everybody in the village. Which could be great, I supposed. It definitely wasn't so good when you wanted to throw filthy pond water on someone and get away with it.

"You remember what Mal did to me, right?" Denny asked.

I nodded. Then I asked, "Which time?" because Denny and Mal Bro had had plenty of arguments.

"He pushed me in the park pond," Denny said. He seemed shocked and offended by my forgetfulness. "You've got to remember."

"But that was ages ago," I said.

"Doesn't matter how long ago it was," Denny told me. "I swallowed so much water I was puking for a month."

I could smell the murky water sloshing in my bucket as I tried to walk in a straight line. I agreed that swallowing even a teaspoon of it would make anyone puke.

Mal's real surname wasn't "Bro". His proper surname was too long and complicated to say all the time. I still thought of Mal as the new kid. Which wasn't totally true because he'd lived in the village since the beginning of Year 7, when we'd all started at the high school. Mal had an older brother called Harry Bro, who was always in trouble, or who was always causing trouble. Most of us younger kids kept well out of his way. To be fair, most of the older kids steered clear of Harry Bro too. Harry Bro was a *trouble magnet*. But that made a lot of us who lived in the village want to avoid Mal too, reckoning he must be the same as his older brother.

Mal and Harry Bro lived on Lindsey Avenue. It was a long road that curved like a backwards C, and they lived in one of the bigger houses halfway along. The lawn at the front of their house was as green as the grass at Pensing Hill Golf Course and I wondered if their dad was a member.

By the time Denny and I got to Lindsey Avenue, we had sore hands and our buckets were only three-quarters full. We'd left splashes and drips all the way from the park.

The whole street was silent. Denny whispered as he told me his plan.

There were two wide upstairs windows at the front of Mal's house. Denny said the one on the left, with the tree outside, was Mal's bedroom window. He said Mal always kept his bedroom window open. I asked Denny how he knew. He said he'd walked past loads of times, making plans for his revenge. I was annoyed I hadn't been included in him making plans but I didn't say so.

"I'm going to climb the tree, OK?" Denny whispered to me. "Then you can pass the buckets up to me."

"Then what?" I asked.

"Then I pour them in the window while he's in bed." Denny laughed but shut up fast and glanced around in case he'd been too loud. He went back to whispering. "Mal may have thrown me *in* the pond, yeah? But now I'm going to throw the pond *onto* him."

"Are you sure this is a good plan?" I asked.

"The best," Denny replied.

I'd promised to help him with his list, so I didn't argue.

We sneaked up Mal's driveway, squeezing past his dad's red BMW, making sure we didn't scratch it with our buckets. I didn't know what kind of tree it was outside Mal's house but it had plenty of thick branches and was easy to climb. Denny was up it in less than a minute.

I lifted the first bucket of pond water as high as I could without spilling it on myself and Denny took it from me. He climbed a branch or two higher so he could reach the bedroom window.

Denny sat astride a thick branch but it still wobbled beneath him, shaking the leaves.

"Careful," I hissed. I stepped back from under the tree in case he fell on top of me.

"Get ready with the second bucket," Denny called down to me as quietly as possible.

Slowly, slowly, Denny squirmed his way along the branch until he was close to the tilted open window. There was a gap in the curtains he was aiming for. The bucket of filthy pond water slopped and dribbled. He had to use both hands to lift it above his head. If he slipped and came crashing down, I knew I should try to catch him – he was my best friend after all.

But Denny didn't fall. He whispered, "Three, two, one." Then he tipped the bucket up, splashing cold and disgusting pond water into the window as well as down the outside of the house. Maybe half the water went into the bedroom if he was lucky.

He dropped the first bucket with a clatter and scurried back along the branch. He hung halfway down the tree, waving frantically for the second bucket. I scrambled a little way up as I passed it to him.

Even from down on the ground I could hear confused and angry noises coming from the upstairs bedroom. There was a lot of swearing.

With gritted teeth, Denny shuffled back along the shaky branch, not seeming to care that he was spilling water from the bucket as he went. This time he rested the lip of the bucket on the very top of the tilted window. And he poured the whole lot inside with a gush.

The swearing from the bedroom was like a volcanic explosion.

The curtains whipped back so fast I thought they might rip. A furious, soaking-wet face appeared at the window. It wasn't Mal. It was his big brother, Harry Bro. He hammered on the window with his fist and glared at Denny with a look that could kill.

More voices and noises were coming from inside. Harry Bro's swearing was so loud it was going to wake the whole house, street, village. I glanced at the second upstairs window and saw Mal staring down at me. He was open-mouthed, confused. And completely dry. Mal pressed his face up against his window to get a better view of what was going on in his front garden. Denny had poured stinking pond water into the wrong bedroom onto the wrong brother.

"Jump!" I shouted to Denny. "Run!"

We left our buckets behind as we legged it.

CHAPTER 5

We made it back to Denny's house without stopping, both sweaty and out of breath from running all the way. Denny's mum wasn't home. She was working the early shift at the supermarket in town. We charged upstairs to his bedroom. This time I sat against the wall with my head between my knees while Denny paced back and forth across the carpet.

Denny was angry that his plan had gone wrong. I was terrified that Harry Bro was going to kill us.

"He'll murder us for what we did," I groaned.

But all Denny said was, "Harry Bro's not going to be able to do anything to me. I'm leaving on Sunday, aren't I?"

"Good for you," I muttered. I was the one who'd still be here and spending all my time checking behind me for Harry Bro. And I wondered if I'd ever see my bucket again. I wasn't going to go back and ask for it.

"Do you think Mal and Harry Bro swapped bedrooms?" Denny asked. "I mean, I'm positive Mal's bedroom was the one with the tree outside. I really am."

"Makes no difference now," I said. I wondered if my mum would let me be home-schooled. That way I'd never have to leave my house ever again.

I noticed Denny hadn't made up any more boxes for moving. The box he'd squashed was still in the middle of the floor.

"You've not packed yet," I said.

"Writing my list was more important," Denny said. He dug in his jeans back pocket and pulled out the crumpled sheet of paper. He scowled as he unfolded it. "I can't believe I failed at the first thing. Maybe we should just go on to number two, yeah?"

"What's number two again?" I asked.

"Re-live my first kiss with Tabby."

I shook my head. "Never going to happen," I said. "What's number three?"

"I can make it happen," Denny said. "I've got a plan."

I rolled my eyes. I was going to ask if his plan for a kiss was any better than his one for revenge. But then a knocking at the front door shocked us both.

We froze.

I mouthed at Denny, *It's Harry Bro.*

The knocking came again. But it didn't sound loud and furious like the hammering fist of an angry murderer.

"It can't be Harry Bro," Denny said. "He doesn't know where I live."

"Everybody knows everything about everybody around here," I said. "Don't answer it."

Denny ignored me. He crept out of his bedroom and stood listening at the top of the stairs. Whoever was outside knocked for a third time. I groaned and followed Denny downstairs, treading softly, step by step. We could see the blurry shape of someone through the front door's patterned glass. They knocked yet again, louder this time, making us both jump.

"Mal could have told his brother where you live," I whispered. Was today the day I was going to die? "Don't answer it," I said again.

The person outside bent down to call through the letterbox. "Denny? It's me. Mal. Are you in? Denny?"

Denny and I sagged with relief.

"What do you want?" Denny shouted.

"Let me in," Mal said. He had his mouth pressed to the outside of the letterbox.

"Mal might have his brother with him," I warned Denny.

"Is Harry Bro with you?" Denny shouted.

"Don't be soft," Mal said. "Why would I want to bring him? What you did was brilliant."

Denny looked at me and shrugged. I shrugged back. So Denny opened the door but checked up and down the lane outside to be sure Mal wasn't lying.

"Brilliant," Mal repeated, shoving his way inside. "Seriously, it was the most brilliant thing ever. You should have seen Harry. Bouncing off the walls. Fuming. Absolute madness."

"He's going to kill us, isn't he?" I said, feeling cold at the idea of being on the wrong end of Harry Bro's heavy fists.

Mal laughed. "Only if Harry finds out who you are. He didn't know who you were, and I said I didn't either."

"You didn't tell him?" Denny asked.

"Why would I?" Mal replied. He looked offended.

I enjoyed the warm feeling of relief. But I also noticed the bruise under Mal's right eye. It was swollen and purple.

"Did your brother do that?" I asked.

Mal touched his eye and winced at the sharp pain. "Not today. This was his present to me on Monday. Harry's got a whole heap of extra homework to do before we go back to school and I refused to do it for him." Mal looked both embarrassed and angry. "Have you got any Coke or something?" he asked Denny, breaking the awkward silence.

The three of us went into the kitchen. Mal was taller than Denny but not as tall as me. He had big ears and eyebrows that met in the middle. He always wore cool T-shirts and expensive trainers. He was also one of the cleverest kids in our year. Maybe in the whole school. And he liked to boast about it too.

There were half a dozen large cardboard boxes stacked on the kitchen floor. Denny's mum was doing her fair share of the packing even if he wasn't. Denny took a large bottle of cola out of his fridge and offered it to Mal. It wasn't proper Coke but the home-brand stuff his mum got from the supermarket where she worked.

Mal didn't complain. He drank it from the bottle. "I'm parched," he told us. "I ran all the way here to catch up with you."

Denny and I often saw Mal and his mates hanging around the park or wherever, but we avoided them. They reckoned they owned the place. Their loud mouths and the way they acted annoyed Denny, causing big arguments and even fights. So me and Denny had stayed away and stuck together, just the two of us.

"Why did you do it?" Mal asked, smiling widely at us again. "Seriously, Harry's bed is drenched. It'll take days to dry out – hopefully."

Denny was the one who looked embarrassed now. He shuffled his feet and mumbled, "It was meant to be you."

"Me?" Mal belched in surprise, cola fumes filling the air. "You were trying to soak me?"

"I was trying to get revenge for when you pushed me in the pond at the park."

"You're kidding?" Mal said. He couldn't believe it. "But that was ages ago. Like nearly two years ago."

"You shoved me in in front of everyone," Denny said. "I'd just got new trainers for my birthday and they were ruined. My mum went wild."

"But it was ages ago," Mal repeated. "I can't believe you're still even thinking about it."

"It was in front of everybody," Denny said again.

"Denny swallowed so much water he was puking for a month," I added, not sure if that helped.

Mal put the cola bottle down on the kitchen counter and held up his hands as if he wanted to make peace. "OK, I'm sorry. Seriously. Whatever." Then Mal asked, "But why do it now?"

Denny pointed at the cardboard boxes his mum had packed. "I'm moving on Sunday. My mum's found a good job, at last. But it's in some place near York."

"Miles away," I said.

"I'd heard you were moving," Mal said. "Andy at the butcher's told Sarah's mum, and she told my mum when she was having her hair done. I didn't know it was so soon. It's really this Sunday? It's going be weird not seeing you around."

"Four days' time," I said, feeling the familiar dread when I thought about it.

I reckoned Denny was wondering how much he could trust Mal. He took out his crumpled sheet of paper from his back pocket.

"I made a list of the things I want to do before I have to leave," Denny said.

Mal read it with a raised monobrow. "I was top of the list? Cool. I'm honoured."

All three of us laughed.

Mal read, "*Re-live first kiss.* I like the sound of that. I bet it was with Marie Martins."

"Tabby Harper," Denny corrected him.

"Seriously? Tabby?" Mal said. "How the hell did you manage that?" He was amazed, but maybe not in a good way. "I don't think she's ever even talked to me. Isn't her dog her best friend? I mean, literally."

"He'll never manage to kiss her a second time," I said, then yelped when Denny punched me, giving me a dead arm.

"I've got a plan," Denny said.

"I'm in," Mal said. He folded Denny's list carefully and gave it back to him. "I'll help. It'll be like my apology for what happened at the pond. If I help you re-live your first kiss with Tabby, then you don't need to get revenge on me. Deal?"

Denny looked at me. He wasn't sure. But I thought that whatever Denny was planning might be easier if there were three of us, including one of the cleverest kids we knew. So I nodded.

Denny eventually nodded too and said, "Deal."

CHAPTER 6

There was both a long way and a short way to walk to Tabby's house. She lived on the road that ran along the back of the high school's playing field. Denny wanted to go the long way, sticking to the roads that zigzagged round the far side of the school. Mal wanted to go the short way, straight across the playing field.

Mal won the argument. And I could tell by the look on Denny's face that he wished he hadn't agreed to let Mal be involved.

There were gangs of seagulls settled on the playing field in the late morning sun. The bright white lines of the football pitch had been freshly marked for the new term starting next week. The high school itself was made of chunky concrete blocks and looked like the world's most boring Lego. Who would I pass the ball to during a game of football when Denny was gone? Whose answers would I copy in tests when Denny was gone? I did my best not to think about it.

Mal listened as Denny explained his plan. "You want to steal Tabby's dog?" Mal said. "Seriously?"

Denny said, "We'll give the dog back again – that's the whole point. Tabby will be so happy and relieved that I *found* her dog that she'll definitely agree to—"

Mal interrupted. "You think the only way you can get a girl to kiss you is by tricking her?"

Denny said, "It's not a trick – it's a *plan*. Totally different."

Mal still had the bottle of cheap cola with him. He shook his head and took a gulp as we walked. "What the hell are you going to do when you want to lose your virginity?" he asked. "Pretend you've rescued orphans from a burning building?"

"Shut up. It's going to work," Denny said. "You think it's a good plan, don't you, Jake?"

I squirmed because Denny was desperate for me to agree with him the same as I always did. But after hearing everything Mal had said,

I wasn't so sure … "I can see both sides," I said, trying to sound like my dad did when talking politics with my mum after she'd had a glass of wine.

Denny looked at me like I was a traitor.

I wasn't a traitor. Denny would always be my best friend and I'd do anything he asked me to. Obviously. But I couldn't help agreeing with Mal and hoping I wouldn't have to kidnap Tabby's dog.

"You're running out of time to do it anyway," I said. "You've been arguing all morning and it's only the second thing on your list."

Mal asked, "Why did Tabby kiss you last time?"

Denny tried his best not to look offended. "Because she wanted to," he said.

"Did she do it as a bet or a dare?" Mal asked.

"Get lost."

"No need to get so uptight about it," Mal said.

"I'm not getting uptight about it," Denny said uptightly. "Tabby isn't the only girl I've kissed, you know? I went out with Julia Creston for, like, a whole month."

Mal raised his monobrow and whistled. "A whole month? Impressive." But he said it in a totally unimpressed voice. "Don't you think this *plan* stuff is all a bit elaborate and over the top? Seriously. Why don't you just ask Tabby if she'll kiss you? Are you trying to blackmail her?"

"What? No," Denny said.

"Are you saying, *Kiss me or I'll kill the dog*?" Mal asked.

"No way. No," Denny replied. And I was pleased he looked shocked at the idea.

"Just ask her then. Up front," Mal said as he swigged more cola. And burped. "She'll either say yes or no."

"And what if she says no?" Denny asked.

"Tough. Move on," Mal told him.

"But Tabby has to say yes," Denny said, waving the piece of paper with his list on it. He stopped walking, planting his feet in the grass. "It's the whole point."

"I reckon the point is not acting like a psycho-cringe-weirdo," Mal told him.

Denny looked angry, shocked and embarrassed all at once. It really twisted up his face. He folded his list and shoved it back into his jeans pocket. He said something that sounded a bit like "Urgh" and stomped off ahead of us across the playing field. A handful of seagulls rose up into the air to avoid him. And I realised Denny was more nervous about asking Tabby for a kiss than he had been of drenching Mal with filthy pond water.

Mal and I followed a few steps behind. Mal offered me the bottle of cola for a swig but I shook my head. I didn't want his backwash.

"Is Denny always like this?" Mal asked.

"Like what?" I asked back.

"Like angry and edgy," Mal replied.

"He doesn't want to move," I said. I lowered my voice. "He's scared, I guess. I would be too."

Mal nodded. "I get it," he said.

I remembered that Mal and Harry Bro had moved here only a couple of years ago.

"Fitting in somewhere new is hard," Mal said. "Especially with a brother like mine who everybody else gets to know very fast, whether they want to or not." Mal shrugged and drank more cola. Then he asked, "What would you have on your list? If you had to leave?"

I hadn't thought about it. I was nervous it could be a very short list of things to re-live and a very long list of things to try to make right.

"I might make one anyway," Mal said. "Even though I'm not leaving."

"Put Harry Bro at number one," I told him. "Revenge for your eye."

"My list would all be about proving I'm nothing like Harry," he said. "No matter what anyone else thinks."

"But you've got loads of mates anyway, haven't you?" I said. "You're always with that gang at the park."

"Not sure I'd call them proper mates," Mal said. "They like that I can pay for them to come bowling or to the cinema or whatever. But none of them would help me if I ever did make a list. Not like you're helping Denny. And I reckon some of them are just using me to get close to my brother because they think he's hard and cool or something."

I didn't say that me and Denny thought Mal acted a lot like Harry Bro sometimes.

"Is your little brother anything like you?" Mal asked.

"Mickey's all right," I said. "I suppose he's not as annoying as most little brothers can be."

"Hey, I'm a little brother!" Mal said, pretending to be offended and making me laugh.

Denny had stopped walking again. I thought me and Mal were going to have to grab him and drag him all the way to Tabby's. But then I saw the reason Denny had stopped dead in his tracks. The tall metal gate across the far side of the field swung open. A white dog trotted through. It was followed by its owner: Tabby Harper. She let the dog off its lead to run as she closed the gate behind herself.

"That's lucky," Mal said. "We don't have to go all the way to her house now, do we?"

I heard Denny swear. "Did you know she was going to be here?" he asked Mal.

"I'm not Mystic Mal the Mind Reader," Mal said. "But I've seen Tabby walking her dog on the field loads of times." He waved and called, "Tabby."

She looked as surprised to see us as we were to see her. But she started walking our way.

Denny swore again. He ran his fingers through his hair. It made no difference whatsoever to his thick curls.

"Ask her," I told him.

"What?" Denny said. "Here? Now? I'm not ready yet."

"Need some breath freshener first?" Mal asked.

Denny looked even more nervous. "What? Do I stink?" He breathed into his cupped hands, inhaled and did it again. "Does my breath really smell bad?" he asked me, and blew in my face.

I recoiled. But only out of normal disgust, not because Denny had bad breath. "You're fine," I told him.

Tabby threw a ball for her dog, Ghost, as she walked towards us. But the dog was more interested in chasing seagulls. He was called Ghost because his fur was so white. I didn't know his breed but he was big and chunky, and

I was even more glad we weren't going to have to kidnap him.

Tabby was quiet at school. I knew some of the other girls called her stuck-up and boring. She went home most lunch-times, saying she had to feed Ghost, so she didn't hang around with them anyway. But I thought Tabby was OK. We'd sat next to each other in Maths last year and she'd never once grassed me up when I used my phone as a calculator. (After I'd lost my phone, my Maths grades went downhill fast.) I supposed she was one of those "wallpaper kids", meaning you didn't always notice they were there.

Tabby had hair like Denny's except her curls bounced rather than clumped. Her brown eyes were much darker. She was also taller than Denny – but who wasn't? I wondered if he'd have to stand on tiptoes to kiss her.

Mal slapped Denny on the back so hard it made him stumble. "Now or never."

"Shut up," Denny replied.

Tabby was wearing a yellow T-shirt and denim cut-off shorts. She smiled when she reached us but she looked puzzled too. "What are you three doing here?"

"Funny you should ask," Mal said.

"Shut up," Denny told him again.

"We were coming to see you," Mal went on.

So then I told Mal to shut up too. This was Denny's moment – good or bad.

Tabby looked even more confused. She said to Denny, "I heard you were moving. Is it on Sunday?"

"That's kind of what I wanted to talk to you about," Denny said.

Ghost was fed up with the seagulls and brought his ball back. Tabby threw it for him.

"Do you ...?" Denny stuttered. "I was thinking, you see ...?"

"Are you OK?" Tabby asked.

Denny pulled his crumpled list out of his back pocket and said to Tabby, "Can I show you something?" He glared at me and Mal standing right behind him, breathing down his neck. "Can I show it to you over here?"

Tabby shrugged and went with Denny, walking a little way across the field.

"She's going to punch him," Mal said. And the gleeful way he said it was one of the reasons I thought he could be as mean as Harry Bro.

I didn't want Denny to get punched. I wanted him to get a kiss. He talked to Tabby in a hurried whisper and I couldn't make out his words. He pointed at his list, waved his hands, tried to laugh, tried to make Tabby laugh. I felt a stab of guilty sympathy for him. Oh god. She really was going to punch him.

Ghost came bounding up to me and Mal, with friendly barks and his pink tongue lolling. The dog dropped his spit-drippy ball at my feet. He barked twice, looking at me with his fluffy white face. *Maybe he should have been called Cloud or Candyfloss*, I thought. I went to pat the dog's head but he jumped back and barked again. So I bent down for his ball. It was slimy and gross. I chucked it for him, then wiped my gunky fingers on my jeans as I watched Ghost chase it.

I flinched when Mal punched my arm. "Ow," I hissed.

"She did it," Mal said, his mouth open and eyes wide. "She did it."

"Did what?" I asked. I looked from Mal to Denny and Tabby again. They were walking back towards us. Tabby was blushing – she had a rosy explosion on each cheek. But Denny had the biggest, hugest, most massive smile on his face I reckoned I'd ever seen.

"She kissed you?" I asked, gutted that I'd missed the big moment.

"She kissed me," Denny said, grinning like he had a surfboard shoved sideways in his mouth.

3 DAYS BEFORE ...

CHAPTER 7

We'd arranged to meet on Thursday morning, on the high-school playing fields again. There were four of us now. Five if you included Ghost. Denny, me, Mal and Tabby sat in a circle on the grass making plans while Ghost chased the seagulls.

Denny's list was getting more and more crumpled. It had begun to tear along one of the unfolded, re-folded, unfolded, re-folded creases.

"You need to laminate that list," Mal told him. He was wearing a denim jacket and took a can of Fanta out of the pocket.

"Who even has a laminator?" Denny asked.

"It's the king of stationery," Mal said. "Seriously. Everyone should have one."

Yesterday, when Denny's mum found out he hadn't even started packing yet, she'd been furious. She'd told him he was not leaving the house until everything he owned was "Inside a bloody cardboard box!"

When I asked Denny earlier if he'd finished packing yet, all he said was, "Getting there."

"I'll help you," I'd told him. "No worries." Because there wasn't long left, was there? I could feel time for our friendship running out and I was a Jake-shaped sponge just trying to soak it up.

Tabby sat on the grass close to Denny so she could read his list. "OK," she said. "I suppose I can understand why you want to apologise to Mrs Hubler."

"I don't want her to think I'm the same little kid I was when I was nine," Denny said. "I want Mrs Hubler to know I've grown up and changed."

"I bet she doesn't believe kids from her class ever grow up," I said. "I bet she makes up her mind about you like that." I clicked my fingers. "And never changes it even if you're eighty-nine."

Tabby was almost touching shoulders with Denny when she leaned over and pointed at the next line on his list. "What did you steal?" she asked. "Was it from a shop or a person?"

Denny squirmed and squinted up at me from underneath his heavy fringe. Which meant Tabby and Mal looked at me too.

"I don't know what it is," I said. "Don't look at me. Denny won't tell me either."

Tabby shrugged. "Big secret. Must be something exciting." She smiled at Denny.

Denny blushed but didn't answer.

Tabby smiled again.

Denny smiled.

Mal smirked and raised his monobrow as he gulped his Fanta.

I reckoned Denny might get to re-live his first kiss yet again before he left.

"So tell me about this horse, then," Tabby said. "Burdock? That's Farmer Clemance's old shire horse, isn't it?"

"Exactly," Denny replied, clearly happy for the subject to change. "But he hates being called *Farmer* Clemance. He says it makes him sound like the bad guy from an Enid Blyton book. I call him Mr Clem."

"He's friends with Denny's mum," I said.

"Yeah, but not in *that* way," Denny said. "He brings her free manure for her roses. It's kind of a thank-you for what I did."

Mal found this hilarious. "Seriously?" he said. "Horse crap as a thank-you? Has no one told him the post office has a whole shelf of greeting cards?"

"My mum loves her roses," Denny said. "She'll probably miss them more than anything else when we move."

Ghost had tired of the seagulls and he flopped himself down next to Tabby. She scratched him between the ears as he panted with his tongue out. "So, what happened with his horse and you?" she asked.

I felt bad for Denny that Mal and Tabby didn't remember. "He was famous," I said.

"Denny or the horse?" Mal asked.

Denny's face flushed angrily. But only for a second. He sighed and looked over at the school buildings across the playing field. "Got to make people remember me somehow. Got to leave my mark."

There was an awkward silence, so I filled it. "You saved its life, really, didn't you?" I said.

"He," Denny said. "The horse, Burdock. He's a *he*."

"But he'd escaped from his field, hadn't he?" I said.

Denny nodded. "Mr Clem reckoned some townie hillwalkers had left the field gate open and—"

"And Burdock was running down the main road, wasn't he?" I said. "Full-tilt galloping." I did the actions of a horse going full tilt, making Mal laugh. "A massive shire horse."

"Burdock was scared of the traffic," Denny said. "It wasn't his fault. And—"

"Cars were swerving, horns were blaring," I said, getting into my storytelling. "You should've seen it. People running and shouting and diving for cover. Then, Denny, he—"

"Who's telling this?" Denny snapped. "Me or you?"

I shut up.

Denny said, "It wasn't Burdock's fault. OK, he's a massive shire horse, but he's not mean. Townie hillwalkers not using their brains left the gate to his field wide open. Burdock wandered out and along the road into the village. Then Mr Clem says something must have spooked him – maybe a car honked its horn or went speeding past him. And Burdock bolted, started running right down the middle of the main road. He really is massive, and people panicked, just making it worse, scaring him even more."

"So what did you do?" Mal asked.

"I was on my bike," Denny said. "I'd gone to the shop for my mum and I saw Burdock running and all those people shouting and making it worse. But, you see, I *knew* Burdock. Because of my mum buying manure for her roses from Mr Clem. I always took carrots and apples to feed him in his field. So, when I saw Burdock galloping towards me, I jumped on my bike and rode alongside him, saying his name and sort of talking to him. And as he slowed down, I patted his neck and stroked him. He stopped running by himself really. I led him into the park and he had a drink at the duck pond."

It was all true. But if Denny had let me tell it, I'd have made it sound much more exciting than he had. Even so, both Tabby and Mal were impressed.

"And you want to do it again?" Tabby asked.

"Sort of," Denny said. "The local paper sent this photographer guy to take my photo. He was only interested if he could get a picture of me sitting on Burdock."

"But Burdock bucked you off," I said. "You broke your arm."

"Only because the photographer annoyed him," Denny said. "He kept jumping around with his camera because he wanted it to look like an action shot, as if Burdock was running or galloping. Mr Clem called the photographer *feckless*. I had to look up what it meant in the dictionary. And like Jake says, I broke my arm. But I never did get my picture in the paper, which is why no one remembers. So I want to ride Burdock down the main road. Then everyone will see me and take loads of pictures."

"Maybe you're the one who's feckless," Mal said, showing off that he knew what the word meant. "And how do you know Mr Clem would let you ride Burdock again anyway?"

Denny shrugged. "It's not like I'm going to ask him first, is it?"

Mal shook his head. "First dogs, now horses. You've got a real thing about kidnapping animals, haven't you?"

"What's that mean?" Tabby asked. Her eyes narrowed with suspicion as she rubbed Ghost's belly.

Denny didn't answer her. He stood up and brushed grass off his jeans. "Burdock's the last thing on my list," he said. "I've got to apologise to Mrs Hubler first."

"I know where she lives," Tabby said.

"Who's going to be scarier?" Mal asked. "Hubler or Burdock?"

CHAPTER 8

"What d'you want us to do if Mrs Hubler murders you?" Mal asked.

Denny would have laughed if he hadn't been so nervous.

The four of us, and Ghost, were on the opposite side of the road to Mrs Hubler's house. We were half hidden beneath two tall horse-chestnut trees. I checked the ground but there were no conkers yet. I wondered if it would still be OK to play conkers in Year 9, or if it was one of those games you were meant to grow out of. Me and Denny had never worried about growing out of stuff. But if he wasn't going to be there any more ...

"Do you think she's home?" Denny asked, staring at the front of the small red-brick bungalow.

"Only one way to find out," Mal told him.

But Denny didn't move at first. And part of me began to think he was going to chicken out. Maybe because that's what I would have done. Denny looked terrified. He looked like he was standing on the highest diving board at the swimming pool in town. But then, I should have known Denny better. Once he had an idea in his head, it was like he found it impossible to forget it or let it go. Denny never climbed back down from the diving board. He always jumped.

"You don't have to do this," I said. "Not if you don't want to."

"I don't want to do it. But I know I have to," Denny said. "Do you know what I mean?"

"Sort of," I said.

"No," Mal said.

"Yes," Tabby said.

Denny clenched his fists down by his sides. Without another word, he strode across the quiet road and opened the low metal gate. He walked up the paved driveway alongside the neat lawn with its ornamental birdbath. Denny hesitated for a only a second, then used the brass knocker to knock at the blue front door.

Mal, Tabby and I held our breaths. Ghost barked, making us jump. Tabby shushed him.

But nobody answered the door. Denny turned to look back at us. All three of us mimed for him to knock again. So he did. I checked up and down the road but I didn't spot any nosey-parkers or curtain-twitchers spying on us from the other houses.

"You still haven't told me why he's doing this," Mal said. He crushed his just-emptied can of Fanta and shoved it in the left-hand pocket of his denim jacket. Then he pulled a new can of Sprite out of the right-hand pocket and popped the tab. He took a swig. "I've never known anyone who's ever wanted to say sorry to a teacher. What was the crime?"

"He drew pictures of her," Tabby said.

"It was graffiti," I added.

Mal looked confused.

"Denny drew pictures of Mrs Hubler on the school walls and in the playground," Tabby said.

"He thought he was just being funny but, looking back, I suppose they were kind of cruel," I said. "The first one he did was on the side of the bike shed and he made Mrs Hubler into the devil with massive horns. And she was eating a cat. Denny didn't admit to anyone except me that it was him who'd drawn it. But he's a good drawer and everyone said it was amazing. So he did more, making her look totally evil, or like some of the bad guys from his favourite comics. He did this one of Mrs Hubler looking like the Joker and it was really, really brilliant. I mean, brilliant but bad, you know? It was in the boys' toilets. Then it just became a weird craze and everybody started drawing nastier and nastier pictures of Mrs Hubler everywhere."

"The whole school had a talk in the assembly hall from the Head," Tabby said. "He told us that what we were doing was bullying. Did you draw any?" she asked me.

I wasn't proud to admit it but I said, "A couple."

Tabby nodded. "Everybody did. Can you imagine having horrible drawings of you everywhere you look? And then the Head got this policewoman to come to school to scare us."

"Threaten us," I said.

Tabby nodded. "Most of it stopped."

"Me and Denny never did any more," I said.

"But Mrs Hubler retired at the end of the term and so it all fizzled out anyway," Tabby said.

A car turned the corner at the top of the road and slowly drove our way. We slunk behind the trunks of the trees until it went by. When we looked back across the road at Mrs Hubler's house, Denny was knocking for a third time.

Mal sipped his Sprite thoughtfully. "Why did Denny do the drawings in the first place?"

"Because Mrs Hubler gave him lines," I said.

"Lines?" Mal pulled a face like the Sprite tasted sour. "What is she? Seriously. A teacher from the 1980s?"

"My mum used to say that Mrs Hubler probably taught Noah how to build his ark," Tabby said. "Because she was definitely the oldest teacher at school. And lines were her favourite punishment. *Write 100 lines of 'I shall not speak in class unless I put my hand up first and ask Mrs Hubler's permission.'*"

I said, "*Write 100 lines of 'I shall leave playtime on the playground as it should never enter the classroom.'*"

Tabby said, "*Write 200 lines of 'I shall always complete all 100 lines given to me because 97 is never enough.'*"

Mal laughed. "We never got any of that at my old school," he said.

"Good for you," Tabby told him.

"Denny reckoned he got lines when it wasn't his fault," I said.

"Well, it wasn't his fault everyone else started doing drawings and turning it into bullying," Mal said. "He shouldn't have to be the one apologising. Or not the only one. You all should."

I looked at Tabby. Tabby stared down at her feet. I prodded the toe of my trainer against the lumpy roots of the trees that had grown up through the pavement. Ghost barked.

"Just saying," Mal said.

Denny gave up and slouched back towards us with his hands in his pockets. "She's not in," he said, stating the obvious.

Part of me was glad Mrs Hubler wasn't home. I wasn't sure if I was brave enough to admit to the things I'd drawn. Maybe one day I would do it – if I ever made a list of my own. But this was Denny's list.

"Should we wait?" Denny asked, looking back across at the silent bungalow. "Maybe she's just gone to the shops?" He blew a lip-flapping mouth-fart of annoyance. "How am I supposed to finish my list if she's on holiday or something?"

We had to get out of Denny's way as he paced round and round the trees. I wasn't surprised he felt annoyed. He'd plucked up the courage, got himself worked up and was ready to dive off that diving board. But it was like the swimming pool had been closed without anyone telling him and now he was left all high and dry.

"Why does everything on my list keep getting messed up?" Denny groaned.

"Thanks," Tabby said.

Denny blushed. "Apart from that. Apart from you, I mean."

"I know," Mal said. "Maybe you should draw a big picture of your sad face with loads of tears and a speech bubble coming out saying *Sorry*." He pointed across at the house. "Do it gigantic on the front wall." Denny scowled at him and Mal swigged his drink. "Just a joke. Seriously."

"We need chalk," Tabby said.

Denny looked shocked. "I'm not doing anything he says," he said, jabbing a finger at Mal.

Tabby shook her head. "No, not that. I think I've got a better idea. Who's got chalk?"

"My little brother's got a tin of chalk at home," I said. "What colour?"

"Every colour," Tabby said.

And then we made plans.

CHAPTER 9

Sneaking out of my house at 2 a.m. was easy.
And it wasn't like it was the first time I'd done it.
I climbed across the garage roof, then dropped
down into the back garden. I crept round the
side of our house, glancing up once at my parents'
window just in case. When I was on the street,
I ran all the way to Mrs Hubler's house, doing
my best to keep out of the streetlights' brightest
patches. My backpack full of my brother's chalks
rattled as I ran. There was a new moon hiding
behind the clouds.

Mal and Denny were already there. They
stood in the shadow of the conker tree on the
opposite side of the road to Mrs Hubler's house.
Mal beckoned and Denny hissed my name until
I spotted them in the dark. Denny had on a
baseball cap pulled low over his eyes, and Mal
was wearing a black balaclava. I ducked under

the low branches next to them. I was wearing my darkest hoodie and I was sweaty after running all the way. The night was still warm even at quarter past two.

"Good news," Denny whispered. "She's not on holiday." He pointed at the white Skoda parked in Mrs Hubler's driveway. It hadn't been there earlier.

I wondered if it really was good news. There was no way she or her husband would be able to catch us if they were on a beach somewhere.

"Where's Tabby?" I asked.

"Probably chickened out," Mal said.

"No way," Denny said. "She's not like that."

Mal turned his head to glance at me. I couldn't see it underneath his balaclava but I reckon he waggled his monobrow. I saw he was drinking Dr Pepper tonight.

"Why are you here anyway?" I asked him. "You didn't even go to our school."

"It's been a really boring summer," he said. "This is the best bit."

"Why are you wearing a balaclava?" Denny asked him.

"Who's wearing a balaclava?" Mal asked.

"You are."

"Am I? How do you know it's me? Seriously. *That's* why I'm wearing a balaclava."

Denny tutted and rolled his eyes.

"I've got loads of chalk," I said, changing the subject. I swung my backpack off my back and unzipped it for them to see.

We were rummaging around for our favourite colours when Tabby showed up.

"Ghost wanted to come with me," she said. "It took a whole packet of bacon to shush him and stop him following me." She saw Mal in his balaclava and asked, "Is that you, Mal?"

"Who knows?" he answered.

And this time we all laughed. But mainly because of our tingling nerves. Being daring and breaking rules gave me an electric thrill. We giggled in hushed little gasps. Was this one of the most daring things we'd ever done?

There were no lights on behind the closed curtains of Mrs Hubler's house. At the front of the red-brick bungalow was a low garden wall. The lawn was cut short, with a square concrete birdbath in the middle. The paved driveway curved up to the blue front door. Our plan was to cover every surface we could. We knew it was going to take us most of the night. But we hoped it was going to be brilliant when we'd finished.

"What if we wake her?" I wanted to know. "Or her husband?"

"Run," Mal said. "Fast. Seriously."

"Then meet up on the school field," Tabby said.

Denny led us out from the cover of the conker tree and across the road to the teacher's house. "Two hundred and fifty each, OK?" he whispered, then opened the garden gate, slowly, slowly.

Mal let out a Dr Pepper burp. It sounded too loud in the silent night.

Denny scowled and put his finger to his lips. Just like a teacher.

Mal whispered, "Sorry," and crumpled his empty can, making even more noise, then he shoved it in his pocket.

I placed my backpack down on the drive and we each took a handful of chalks. Then we got to work.

We wrote in bold letters and colourful letters. Jagged letters and curly letters. Some letters half a metre tall. We wrote on the driveway, the garden wall, even on the walls of the house itself. All you could hear was our nervy breathing and the scritching, scratching of our chalks. We all kept checking for movement at the dark windows, watching for the slightest twitch of a curtain. But we truly were the most silent scribblers you could imagine. We each wrote the same sentence two hundred and fifty times. Over and over again. Our clothes were covered in rainbow dust. Our hands ached. Now and again we stood back to admire our work. It was like nothing any of us had ever seen before.

It took us until after 5 a.m. But it didn't ever feel like work and definitely wasn't like punishment. I picked up my backpack and followed the others as we tiptoed across the road and snuck back under the branches of the conker tree. It was still dark but, even so, the effect of our writing was eye-popping.

We'd covered the front of the house, the garden wall, the driveway and even the birdbath. Everywhere. *Everywhere!* In every colour.

Yesterday I'd told Denny that Mrs Hubler wouldn't forgive him even if he said sorry a hundred times. But how about a thousand?

I am sorry, Mrs Hubler.

"What more proof does she need?" Denny asked.

CHAPTER 10

"What do you reckon Mrs Hubler's going to say when she sees it?" Mal asked as we stood and looked at our handiwork. His black balaclava had turned multicoloured with chalk dust and he sounded kind of shocked by what the four of us had done. I knew how he felt. But it was too late to take it back now.

"I hope it doesn't rain or she'll never see it," Tabby said. "It'll all wash away."

"It's one of the coolest things I've ever done," Mal said. "Top five, easily. My brother would never do anything like this. Harry would just chuck rocks at the windows."

"I'm glad you're not him," Denny said.

"We all are," I said.

"Go knock on her door," Mal told me.

"You go knock on her door," I replied.

Mal shrugged. "OK."

But Denny stopped him. "We've got to wait until it's light. It'll look even better then."

We walked to the park. Denny and Tabby walked ahead of me and Mal, close together. I told myself I didn't mind because I knew he was going to miss me more. But I still didn't have a clue what I was going to do when Denny went. The loneliness that was coming gave me a knot in my gut that felt like it was being pulled tight by frosty hands.

We made our way to the play area. Me and Tabby sat on the swings while Denny perched on the bottom of the slide opposite us and grinned at the chalk covering his hands. Mal sprawled backwards on the wooden roundabout. He stared up at the lightening sky as he kicked himself lazily round and around. We re-lived our night of daring line-writing, laughing at our scares when a car went by or a cat meowed, making us all jump. None of us talked about Denny leaving. And that was good.

At one point, Mal got up and wandered over to the duck pond. He tried to wash his balaclava in the chilly water but the chalk dust clumped up and turned a disgusting brown colour. He ended up throwing the balaclava in a litter bin.

"Are you sure you're the cleverest kid in our year?" Tabby asked him, making us all laugh.

Denny only stopped giggling when I said, "Today's the day you give back that thing you stole. That's next on your list, right?"

Mal walked back over to the roundabout. "You still not going to tell us what it is?"

"Later," Denny said.

The four of us sat together and watched the sun rise over the village. We didn't talk. We just enjoyed it.

It was just before seven o'clock when Denny said, "Come on. Let's go back to Mrs Hubler's."

As we walked back the way we'd come, we argued about who should knock on Mrs Hubler's door and wake her up. Both Denny and Mal wanted to do it. So when we turned onto her road, the last thing we expected was to see a small crowd of people at Mrs Hubler's front gate. There were several of her neighbours, two or three of them wearing pyjamas.

Mal said, "Uh-oh."

Tabby swore.

But there was no way we could stop ourselves from wanting to get closer and see what was happening.

We stayed on the opposite side of the road and tried to act casual. We made it back under the conker tree. Denny had been right – those big, bold, colourful, swirling one thousand lines looked amazing in the sunlight.

Mrs Hubler and her husband were standing in their dressing gowns in their garden. They had their backs to us as they stared at our multicoloured letters and words and lines covering the front of their house and garden wall and driveway. We couldn't hear what they were saying. Mrs Hubler waved her hands in front of her like she was conducting an unruly orchestra. Her grey hair was frothy and wild. Mr Hubler had his hands gripping the top of his bald head as if they were superglued on.

"I've got to get a photo of this," Mal said, whipping out his phone. "Seriously."

Tabby did the same. Denny too.

Yet again I reckoned it was rubbish that I was thirteen and phoneless.

Mrs Hubler started trying to shoo away her neighbours. I guessed she must feel odd having her house as this peculiar centre of attention. Yet she didn't look angry. She looked amazed. Gobsmacked. Some of her neighbours were laughing. But that was when she turned and saw us on the other side of the road, and all four of us tried to hide behind the tree at the same time, bumping into each other.

"Is this you?" Mrs Hubler shouted. "Did you do this?"

Her neighbours and husband turned to look at us too. Bald Mr Hubler just looked like a big, confused baby.

"Walk," Mal hissed. "Go. Move. Quick." He pushed the three of us in front of him along the pavement.

We ducked our heads and turned our backs. I was praying nobody recognised us or noticed the smudges of chalk dust on our clothes. We didn't run. But we walked back the way we'd come very, very fast.

CHAPTER 11

We were on top of the world and we couldn't stop grinning and laughing. Mrs Hubler had been amazed, astonished. Not angry. Mr Hubler had been flabbergasted. We clapped each other on the back and punched the air. We bounced along. It was like we'd won some incredible prize.

We stopped on the corner of the main road, where we had to split up to go our separate ways. Mal pulled his phone out of his pocket to look at his photos. Tabby and Denny did the same, and we huddled round to see. Tabby had a brilliant shot of Mr Hubler holding his bald head that made us laugh hardest of all.

Denny swiped through his photos. He pointed at the lines he'd written on the wall and driveway. He boasted about how big, giant, enormous his letters were.

"Send the photos to me," I said. No way did I want to miss out just because I didn't have a phone. "You'll email them to me, won't you?"

"I might go back and take some more pictures before it rains," Mal said. "Coolest idea ever," he told Tabby.

She had purple and orange chalky splotches on her cheeks and fingers. "I need to wash this off before my mum sees."

"Not yet," Mal said. "We're on a roll. Come on, Denny. What's next on your list?"

Denny shoved his phone in his pocket. He shook his head as he glanced at me.

"I've got to get home," I said. "Before my mum and dad get up and see I've snuck out."

"Don't be so boring," Mal groaned. "You've got to give back what you stole, right, Denny? That's what's next on your list."

"Later," Denny said. He started walking again and Mal scooted along beside him.

"It has to be something big that you stole," Mal said. "Or you wouldn't be so guilty about it. Was it a car?"

"What?" Denny was appalled. "Of course not."

"A bike?" Mal pushed.

Denny kept walking, shaking his head. We trailed after him.

"Trainers?" Tabby asked. "Did you steal new trainers once when you were in town?"

"Some comics?" I asked. Because I couldn't think of anything I'd seen that he'd got new recently – apart from his phone.

"Did you steal this thing from a shop?" Mal asked. "Or from school?"

"No! Shut up," Denny said, hunching his shoulders as he walked faster. I noticed he still had his hand in his pocket as if he was clutching his phone. "I'll do it later," he said.

"Was it just money?" Tabby asked.

"I know!" Mal shouted. He grabbed Denny's arm to yank him back and stop him running off. He shoved Denny towards Tabby and said, "A heart. You stole someone's heart."

Both Tabby and Denny cringed and Tabby punched Mal in the arm. But Mal waggled his monobrow and laughed.

"Your phone," I said. I thought I was being so clever to have worked it out. "You stole your phone."

It was obvious I was right because of the expression on Denny's face. He wasn't annoyed or embarrassed. His guilt flashed in his eyes as bright as the blue lights on a police car. He couldn't hide it. Mal and Tabby watched with open mouths as Denny pulled the phone out of his pocket.

"Where did you get it?" Mal was excited with the mystery. "Who did you nick it from?"

"It looks like your old phone, Jake," Tabby said to me. She knew exactly what phone I used to have because she'd seen me use the calculator app loads of times when we'd sat next to each other in Maths. I was always sneaking it out under the desk when Mr Latchmore turned his back.

"Same make and model, that's all," I said.

I looked at Tabby but she didn't want to meet my eyes. So I looked at Mal and he frowned down from behind his monobrow. They'd worked it out much faster than I had.

"I'm thirsty," Mal said. "I might go home and get a drink."

"I'll come with you," Tabby said. But they didn't move.

"My phone had a red-and-gold cover, not silver-and-black," I told them.

Denny pulled the cover off the phone and held it out to me.

"I'm sorry I stole it," he said.

ONLY 2 DAYS UNTIL ...

CHAPTER 12

My parents weren't awake yet and didn't know
I'd snuck out. They didn't know I had my phone
back either. I chucked it into the corner of
my bedroom. Hard. I didn't care if the phone
smashed. I took off my chalk-dusted clothes and
pushed them into the bottom of my wardrobe.
Then I sprawled on my bed, but I couldn't fall
asleep, even though I'd been up all night and was
beyond exhausted.

Denny had stolen my phone. My best friend
had lied to me.

How did I feel when he'd given it back to me?
Stupid. And raw, like Denny had used a cheese
grater on my insides. I hurt.

Later that morning my mum tried to get me
out of bed but I told her I had a stomach ache. It
didn't feel like a lie. I was gutted. Mum admitted

I looked pale and left me alone with a cup of tea, a plate of dry toast and a washing-up bowl next to my bed in case I needed to puke. I pulled my duvet over my head and sank down as low as I could go.

I went over and over things in my head. Just spinning never-ending spiralling thoughts. Didn't Denny understand how much trouble I'd been in when I'd had to tell my mum I'd lost my phone? It had been the most expensive thing I'd ever owned. And it had disappeared.

But how come I hadn't even realised how weird it was that I'd lost my phone one day, then Denny had got the exact same make and model only a few days later? It wasn't surprising he'd said he didn't have a contract, because there was no way he could use my number. He'd bought himself a different colour cover and lied, lied, lied. Was having a phone more important to Denny than having my friendship?

I wanted to grab him, shake him and ask him that exact question.

I never wanted to talk to him again.

I wanted to get Denny to tell me why.

I wanted to ignore him for ever.

But he was my best friend, my only friend, and all these thoughts made me curl up around my aching belly.

I punched and punched my pillow, pretending it was his face. Denny was moving away the day after tomorrow and it was like he'd already gone and I was already alone.

CHAPTER 13

It was after midday when I finally crawled out of bed. I draped my duvet around me like a cloak and tramped downstairs. The house was quiet. Mum was at work. Dad and my brother Mickey had driven into town to get him some new shoes for school on Monday. I found a note from Dad on the kitchen table. His handwriting was terrible and I always struggled to read his notes. In his loopy letters Dad had written:

Denny phoned twice, then came round looking for you. It must be important?! I said you weren't feeling well. He said for you to get in touch with him as soon as you can.

I read the note twice. It bugged me the way Dad often used *?!* I didn't even know what it meant. I put the note back on the table and went to the fridge looking for food. Last night's leftover Hawaiian pizza was perfect. I didn't even bother to shove it in the microwave, just started eating it cold.

The doorbell rang. I guessed it might be Denny and so did my best to ignore it. But it rang again, twice. Still wearing my duvet, I went into the living room and sneaked a look through the window. I was surprised to see Tabby and Ghost at the front door. She must have noticed me out of the corner of her eye and turned to look my way. I was too slow to duck back. Tabby waved, then rang the doorbell again. Swearing under my breath, I went to let her in.

"What?" I asked as I opened the door.

"We're worried about you," Tabby said.

"Who's worried?" I said. "You and Ghost?" I stroked the dog's head.

"All of us," Tabby said. "Even Mal."

I sighed to prove how miserable and fed up I was, but I let Tabby and Ghost into the house. I went back into the kitchen to finish my cold pizza and they followed me.

"Has Denny sent you to talk to me?" I asked.

"I wanted to come anyway," Tabby said. "I told him I'd come. And he's really scared you won't talk to him at all any more."

"Good," I said. "I never want to speak to him ever again," I lied.

I sat down at the table and took a bite of pizza. Tabby watched me. Ghost watched the pizza. I gave Ghost the pizza and it disappeared in a single chomp. Then he lay down on the kitchen floor with his tongue out.

Tabby stayed standing. "Denny really is sorry," she said.

"Are you his girlfriend now?" I asked.

She looked surprised by the question. "No," she said. "We're just friends."

"You kissed him," I said.

"So? It was on his list. I might have kissed you too if you'd asked."

Now Tabby surprised me. She only shrugged when I squinted up at her.

She said, "We've promised to keep in touch when Denny leaves, that's all."

"How's he going to keep in touch with you if he's not got my stolen phone?" I didn't care how spiteful I sounded.

Tabby fidgeted and shuffled some more. "Will you talk to him?" she asked.

"What about? There's nothing to say, is there? And then he'll be gone anyway."

"Denny's still got one thing left to do on his list," Tabby said. "Mal and I are going to help him."

"Help him all you want," I told her. "No way is he ever going to be able to ride that horse."

"Maybe he could if you helped too."

"Why should I help him do anything?" I asked.

I could tell that Tabby understood how I was feeling. So I was annoyed she still wanted to make peace. "But you've been friends for so long," she said. "You're his best friend."

"Maybe I wish Ghost was my best friend," I said. I leaned down to stroke his white head. "Just like he's yours."

Tabby stared at her dog but her eyes seemed to look right through him. "Human friends might be nice sometimes," she said.

There was a long moment of silence and I didn't know if I was meant to reply or not.

With a jolt, Tabby popped back into herself. "But Ghost's definitely the best friend ever, ever, ever." And she buried her face in the dog's snowy fur. "Yes, you are. Yes, you are." She tickled his belly.

As I watched them, I thought again about how I'd hardly ever seen Tabby hanging around with other girls in our class. At break-time, she often sat alone, reading. And I knew the reason that me and Mal had thought she'd be impossible for Denny to kiss wasn't because Tabby was popular or had a cool reputation. More like the opposite.

Thinking that Tabby might be lonely too made my eyes feel hot and prickly. But no way did I want her to see me cry.

I jumped to my feet. "You've got to go," I said. "My mum and dad won't be happy if they come home and see Ghost in their kitchen." It was a lie. I just wanted her gone.

Tabby tugged on Ghost's leash to get him to stand, then I led them down the hall to the front door.

"You're not really going to throw your friendship with Denny away, are you?" Tabby asked.

I pushed my knuckles into my eyes to try to keep the tears back. I wanted to say it was Denny who'd done the throwing away.

"He'll miss you so much," Tabby said.

I already had the door open and pushed Tabby outside, slamming it so fast after her that I almost trapped Ghost's tail. I ran upstairs to my bedroom. I hated myself for wanting to cry. I hated Denny for making me want to cry. I refused to cry. I punched my pillow instead of crying.

My phone was on the floor in the corner of my room where I'd thrown it earlier. I still had no idea how I was meant to explain to my parents that I'd found it again. There was a big part of me that didn't want to tell them Denny had stolen it. And that felt strange because it meant I was trying to remain loyal to him.

His friendship had tough hooks in me.

I grabbed my phone and climbed onto my bed, curling up and pulling the duvet over my head again. It seemed like Denny had deleted everything from the phone that had been mine. All my texts and WhatsApps from before last Christmas had gone. My uncle's and cousins' phone numbers had been replaced with the numbers of people Denny knew. But that was useless because he didn't even use it to call anyone.

I pressed the icon on the screen to open the photo gallery. There were the pictures Denny had taken of Mrs Hubler's house covered in our one thousand lines. And a picture of the buckets of pond water we'd meant to throw on Mal. There was also the selfie we'd taken in the bunker at Pensing Hill Golf Course.

But there were loads more. He'd taken photo after photo of the two of us. Sneaky ones in Geography class when we'd been bored. Smiling ones he'd taken when his mum had treated us to a KFC in town. Several from my birthday at the bowling alley. Lots of Denny's birthday when we'd gone paintballing.

As I flicked through, I was surprised to see he'd kept all of the old photos that I'd taken too. There were hundreds. Me and Denny grinning.

Me and Denny laughing. Climbing trees and riding bikes and running around and leaping about and acting up and going wild. And being best friends.

I switched the phone off. I still couldn't forgive him. And he was leaving anyway. So what did it matter?

THE LAST DAY

CHAPTER 14

The doorbell rang at nine o'clock on Saturday morning. And rang. And rang. Like someone was leaning on it. I heard my mum answer it with a grumpy, "Yes, yes, for goodness' sake!" I knew she'd still be in her pyjamas and dressing gown. Saturday mornings were lazy mornings at our house.

I thought it might be Denny. But I hoped it would be Tabby.

Mum called upstairs, "Jake? Malcolm's here for you."

"Who?" I called back.

"Mal Bro," Mum replied.

I was suspicious. Had Denny sent Mal?

I'd spent all yesterday curled up alone, but feeling sorry for myself got boring after a while. Loneliness even more so. Was this what I had to look forward to without Denny? I'd been trying to decide if I'd rather shout at him instead of ignoring him, or punch him instead of avoiding him. I'd looked at all the photos on my phone over and over again. I still hurt so badly that I reckoned forgiving him was one hell of a steep mountain to climb.

Mal was waiting for me in the front garden. He was on his bike, rocking the pedals back and forth. And because it was Mal, of course it was a top-of-the-range bike with probably a hundred gears or something. He was drinking Pepsi Max. He grinned at me and waggled his monobrow.

"You're going to want to see this," Mal told me. "Seriously."

He saw the suspicious frown on my face.

"*Double* seriously," he said. "Get on. I'll give you a pag."

I shouted to my mum that I was going out and slammed the door after me. Mal called it a "pag", while I called it a "backie" – same difference. I climbed onto his bike's seat, wobbled and grabbed handfuls of his T-shirt at his waist. Mal gave me his can of Pepsi Max to hold, so then I could only grab him with one hand. He stood up on the pedals and picked up speed as we headed out onto the road.

"Is it Denny?" I shouted in his ear as we sped along.

"Who else?" he replied.

"Is he riding Burdock?" I asked. "Is he really doing it?"

Mal didn't answer.

It was another hot morning. We bumped and bounced over the dodgy potholes, my legs swinging free and wide on each side of the bike. The Pepsi Max fizzed all over me. I could have thumped Mal on his back and told him to drop me off but I was way, way too curious. Riding Burdock was the last thing on Denny's list.

I bunched up Mal's T-shirt even tighter in my fist. "Has he kidnapped the horse?"

Still no answer.

We headed for the main road. Mal sped around the corner by the church and bounced us up onto the pavement. Beyond the post office was a small stretch of shops. There was the hairdresser's, bakery, chemist, Spar and what my mum called the "tat shop" because it sold everything from herbal tea to fake flowers and wind chimes. The war memorial and the Hat and Hare pub were on the opposite side of the road next to the main entrance to the park.

Tabby was waiting for us with Ghost on his leash in front of the war memorial. Mal jammed on his brakes, skidding to a stop in front of Tabby. I yelped and slid forward off the bike seat as he did, slamming into his back. Pepsi Max went everywhere. Ghost barked at us but Tabby only rolled her eyes and tutted.

"Told you I'd get Jake to come," Mal said to Tabby.

"You didn't give me much choice," I said as I clambered off his bike. Then to Tabby I added, "Has Denny really kidnapped Mr Clem's horse?"

She shook her head. "He got permission."

"She persuaded him to get permission," Mal added, taking his can back and frowning at how much I'd spilled.

"We all went to see Mr Clem yesterday afternoon," Tabby said. "And after Denny had explained everything, Mr Clem said Denny could ride Burdock this morning, before there's too much traffic around. And as long as Mr Clem leads them."

I got a twinge of jealousy that the three of them had been together yesterday afternoon while I'd been feeling sorry for myself.

"I tried to tell Denny it's just going to be total cringe," Mal said. "Seriously. He's going to look like a right muppet riding that massive horse down the road."

"But it's on his list," Tabby said. "The last thing."

"When Denny gets an idea in his head, he never lets it go," I said. I turned to look beyond the pub, up the road to where it bends sharply before carrying on past the high school. That was the way to Mr Clem's farm and the way Denny would come. "What time's he meant to be here?"

"Any time now," Tabby said.

Our main road was never truly busy and only ever came to life on Saturday mornings, so Denny had chosen the right time to be seen. There were handfuls of people about, popping in and out of the shops.

Mal, however, wasn't looking along the road; he was looking across it at the shops on the opposite side. "Uh-oh," he said.

Tabby and I turned to see what was wrong. "Uh-oh, what?" Tabby asked.

"My brother," Mal said.

Harry Bro had ambled out of the bakery, stuffing his face with a sausage roll. He'd spotted Mal and was crossing the road towards us. He ignored the car that honked its horn as he stepped off the pavement in front of it.

Harry Bro looked like his younger brother, but only if a tank looked like a tricycle or a mountain looked like a molehill.

I bent down to stroke Ghost, half turning away. I was nervous Harry might recognise me from three days ago when Denny had chucked pond water over him. Mal reckoned Harry Bro had only got a good look at Denny but I didn't want to take any chances.

So I was more than happy when Harry Bro ignored both me and Tabby. "You got any money?" he asked Mal.

Next to his older, meaner brother, Mal Bro seemed to shrivel. "What for?" Mal said.

Harry Bro stuffed the rest of the sausage roll in his mouth and swallowed without chewing. "I'm still hungry," he said. "And you've always got money. Dad always gives you more than me."

"That's not true," Mal said.

Harry Bro reached out and started patting his younger brother's jeans pockets. "Cough up. Come on," Harry said. Mal was holding his bike in one hand and his can of drink in the other and couldn't move away. Harry Bro's pats became punches, as if he was trying to give Mal a dead leg. "Don't make me take it from you. Not in front of your little friends. That'd be embarrassing."

"OK, OK. Just a minute," Mal said, and gestured for me to hold his bike. "I need another drink anyway," he said to his brother. "But you're only getting a sausage roll. Seriously. Nothing else, OK?"

"I knew you'd be loaded," Harry Bro said with a twisted grin.

The two of them wandered back across the road towards the bakery. Harry Bro walked with great strides like he owned the world. Mal walked like he wished the world would swallow him up.

"I feel sorry for Mal," Tabby said. "No one deserves a brother like that."

"I hope he's gone before Denny gets here," I said.

But no such luck. Because that was when we heard the slow clopping of heavy hooves.

CHAPTER 15

Living all the way out in the country where we did, no one was surprised to see horses and their riders. At first, not many people took much notice of Denny as he came clopping along on the back of Burdock. Denny, however, must have reckoned he looked like the king of the village. He even waved and shouted "Hello!" at the few shoppers on the high street who had paused to give him a second glance.

Mr Clem was a tall man in black wellies, a green woolly jumper and a leather flat cap. He led Burdock with a rope and was nowhere near as tall as his horse, who was black and grey, magnificent and proud. Denny looked like he was clinging on for dear life yet loving every minute of it. As they clopped past the pub, I could see there was a line of slow-moving cars trapped behind them.

They drew level with me and Tabby standing next to the war memorial. I had to crick my neck back to look at Denny all the way up there on the horse.

"Jake," Denny called. "I did it. I'm riding Burdock!"

He shouted it like I couldn't see with my own eyes. And I wanted to wave back and cheer. It was my first instinct. But I told myself to remember that he'd stolen my phone. I had to remind myself that we weren't friends any more. So I only nodded at him. I was still holding Mal's bike and kept my hands gripping the handlebar grips. I didn't smile – I had to force myself not to.

Tabby waved at Denny. I could tell she thought it was hilarious but in a good way. "List complete," she shouted. "You did it."

Denny grinned wider and wider. More of the people on the street were beginning to recognise the oddness of what they were seeing and stopped to watch. Some of them waved at Denny too. He loved waving back. Faces appeared at the hairdresser's window, staring out. One or two passers-by pointed their phones at Denny and Burdock, snapping photos. Denny was lapping it up.

He didn't see Mal and Harry Bro come out of the bakery.

I did.

Denny didn't spot Harry Bro's scowl. He didn't realise that Harry Bro had recognised him.

But I did.

And maybe if Denny had seen the flash of rage that crossed Harry Bro's face he would have been as terrified as I was.

It all happened so fast. Harry Bro already had his second sausage roll in his mouth and he clenched his teeth so hard he bit it in two. One half of the sausage roll fell to the pavement as he raged. Mal tried to grab his brother's arm and drag him away but there was no stopping him. Harry Bro sent Mal sprawling backwards into the bakery.

"I see you," Harry Bro shouted at Denny. He swore and jabbed a threatening finger. "Bucket Boy! I see your face."

That was when Denny saw Harry Bro. And Denny shut up, stopped waving and went as white as Ghost.

Mr Clem was on the wrong side of Burdock to see what all the fuss was about. He kept going, continuing to lead the horse and Denny through the village.

Harry Bro bent down and snatched up a stone from the road. I could see the fire in his eyes even from where I was standing with Tabby. He wound back his arm like a baseball pitcher and threw the stone with all his strength. Harry Bro had a lot of strength. When it hit Burdock's rump, the poor horse must have thought it was a bullet.

Burdock reared and roared, sounding more like a wounded bear than a horse. Denny cried out but somehow managed to cling on. It took Mr Clem by surprise and the rope was yanked from his hands.

Harry Bro laughed. Tabby swore. Ghost barked. Burdock bolted. Shoppers dived for safety into shop doorways. And I jumped on Mal's bike to chase after Burdock and Denny.

Burdock may have been old and heavy but he was fast. I powered the bike's pedals round and round trying to catch up. Mr Clem tried to follow but he was far too slow in his wellies. Denny was thrown about on the horse's back like he was riding the world's scariest bucking bronco. He was tossed up and down and side to side. He was going to get thrown off any second. And what did I think I was going to do? Catch him?

The horse charged along the main road past the post office and the church, past the sign at the edge of the village that read "Thank You For Driving Carefully".

We sped past Pensing Hill Golf Course in a blur. There were just fields, hedgerows and trees on both sides. But I was catching up. As I drew level, I could see Burdock's big brown eyes were wide and rolling. His hooves sounded like thunder on the road.

I reckon I was clinging as tightly to Mal's bike as Denny was to the horse. I tried to call to Denny but he was like a rag doll being tossed around on Burdock's back. His hair blew across his face so he couldn't even see where Burdock was going. Something white and creased was flapping out of his jeans back pocket. It was his list. As I watched, I saw the wind tug at it, pull it free and fling it into a hedgerow at the side of the road.

I had to get as close as I could. But Burdock was like a black-and-grey juggernaut of dangerous muscle and flashing legs. If he rammed into me hard enough, he'd put me into a hedgerow or slam me into a tree or even trample me into the tarmac. I pedalled harder, desperate to keep up.

I knew I had to reach out to grab his rope and rein him in. But I was going so fast I didn't dare take a hand off the handlebars. I could hear Denny panicking and shouting. I could hear Burdock's pounding hooves. I could hear my own ragged, gasping breath. It felt like I was pedalling so fast, Mal's bike might disintegrate beneath me.

I didn't see the small red car coming towards us until too late. It swerved to avoid Burdock at the last second and I saw the gobsmacked face of the old man driving.

Burdock swerved too. But I didn't react fast enough and the horse barged into me. I bounced off all that solid muscle. The bike shuddered and wobbled beneath me. The handlebars juddered and twisted. Somehow I held on. Somehow I managed not to crash.

But I'd been forced to slow down and had to pedal even harder to catch up again. I was sweating, zapped of breath. Yet Burdock could probably have run on for miles and miles – all day long if he'd wanted to. I couldn't tell if the hammering noise was Burdock's hooves or my heart. Denny was still yelling. If he was thrown off Burdock, he'd break more than his arm this time.

When I caught them up again, I knew it was now or never.

"Easy, Burdock," I panted. "You're OK. Easy. You're OK."

I reached for the rope with one hand as it whipped around in the wind. I snatched for it. Missed. Tried again.

And caught the rope. And held tight. So tight.

I put both hands back on the handlebars again and took my feet off the pedals. I let Burdock pull me along.

The big horse dragged me fast at first. I whizzed along the country road, the white lines zooming beneath my wheels. But as I talked to Burdock, he began to get slower, then slower. Gradually, I could feel him calm and canter, then trot.

I kept hold of his rope as Burdock slowed to a walk. As soon as the horse stopped altogether, Denny sort of jumped, sort of tumbled down. His legs buckled on the road and he staggered a few shaky steps. Then he bent double, collapsed to his knees and puked against a tree.

I wished I had my phone to take a photo.

DAY ZERO

CHAPTER 16

The sky was cloudy on Sunday morning. It felt chilly because it was the end of the summer. It had rained last night, so I guessed Mrs Hubler's house would be washed clean of all our chalk lines and back to normal.

My plan that morning was to stand on the corner of Denny's lane and watch him leave. Tabby and Mal had said they'd be there too. I still didn't think I wanted to talk to Denny. But I just knew there was no way I could stay at home, holed up in my bedroom, while Denny and his mum drove away from our village for ever. But Denny had other plans.

The first surprise was the big bag of fresh manure that had been left in our front garden. Not that my mum knew what on earth to do with it because she didn't enjoy gardening as much as

Denny's mum. But it was the thought that counts, right?

The second surprise was Denny himself. I left my mum and dad to deal with Mr Clem's manure gift and I walked down our road. Looking up, I saw Denny waiting for me at the far end. He stood with his hands in his pockets, shuffling his feet but obviously determined to talk to me. I stopped when I reached him and we both stood there with our hands in our pockets, shuffling our feet.

At last I said, "I bet your mum's going a bit wild wondering where you've disappeared to."

Denny shrugged. "She'll probably guess. But the removals van's nearly packed and we're meant to follow them."

So the two of us walked across the village towards Denny's house.

"You didn't stay yesterday," Denny said. "I wanted to say thanks for saving me, I really did, but you went."

"It felt weird," I said. Which was true. All these people had suddenly crowded around and made me feel claustrophobic. I hadn't wanted them all taking photos of me. When Mr Clem had arrived, I'd handed him Burdock's rope and tried to get away. But packs of people had followed us along the main road, some in their cars, and everyone was over-excited and fussing.

I'd given Mal his bike back when I'd spotted him and Tabby in the crowd. He'd told me I was awesome, which was cool. But as more people had turned up it had been easier for me to sneak away. I'd left Mal and Tabby with Denny as I'd walked home.

On my way, I'd spotted a square of crumpled, dirty white paper stuck in a hedgerow. It had been flapping in the breeze as if it had wanted me to see it. I'd plucked it from between the hedge's branches. Now I remembered I still had it in the back pocket of my jeans.

"This is yours," I said to Denny, handing him his list.

He stared down at it as we walked along the main road. "I reckon you'll be the one best remembered now, right? The kid who stopped the runaway horse?"

"We've both done that now," I said.

Denny nodded, shrugged. "But I really did want to change things and make things better too," he said. "And I ended up making stuff worse." He scrunched his list up, didn't fold it.

Even now I hated it when Denny looked miserable. "You didn't make it *all* worse," I said. "Mal and Tabby are both really cool."

"I made it worse with you."

I went quiet again.

"I'm really sorry, Jake. Really, really sorry."

"Me too."

"You'll never forgive me, will you?" he asked.

"You were meant to be my best friend," I said.

We turned the corner onto Denny's lane. At the far end stood his mum's car and a red-and-white removals van parked up outside his house. His *old* house. Denny's mum was at the garden gate, hands on her hips, oozing impatience. She was even shorter than Denny but had the same messy, curly hair.

Mal, Tabby and Ghost were there too and Tabby saw us first, pointing our way. Denny's mum threw her hands in the air and beckoned him to hurry up.

"At least you won't be on your own at school tomorrow," Denny said. He meant I'd have Tabby and Mal. "I hope I meet new friends just like you three."

The removals van started up, its engine loud on a quiet Sunday morning in the middle of nowhere. I hoped Denny had managed to pack all his drawings and comics, dead wasps' nest and Dave the Venus flytrap.

"Got to go," he said. But before he did, he dug in his jacket pocket and pulled out a phone. It was a different make and model to mine. "Mum got me this. So we can keep in touch." He hesitated, took a breath. "If you want."

I gripped my own phone in my pocket.

"Call me?" Denny asked.

"No." I shook my head. "You call me."

"OK," he said. "I will." Then he took off, running down the lane to his impatient and fretting mum.

Denny ran past Tabby, Mal and Ghost, shouting goodbye and waving. His mum bustled him into the car. It was an old banger and I crossed my fingers that it would make it as far as wherever they were going. The removals van moved away from the kerb and eased around the front of the car. I watched it trundle past me. It had "Kingdom Move" in huge red letters on the side with the picture of a king piece from chess.

Denny's mum drove close behind the van. She waved at me through the windscreen but before I could wave back I saw Denny insisting she pull the car over. She wasn't happy about it but stopped the car beside me. Denny wound down his window and I walked over as he leaned out.

He had his list in his hand. "You can keep it if you want."

I was surprised. But I took it. And I was even more surprised that, yes, I did want to keep it.

"What is it?" his mum asked.

"Nothing," Denny said. Then he changed his mind and grinned. "Everything."

They drove away and turned the corner.

I opened the list and smoothed it out while I waited for Mal, Tabby and Ghost. I'd told Denny his list was impossible. But everything I'd said he couldn't do, he'd gone and done anyway.

My friends walked up to meet me. Tabby kissed me on the cheek, Ghost barked and Mal offered me a swig from his can.

The list of thank-yous

Jasmine and Clara who are brilliant at providing everything an author needs (food, space, ears, encouragement); Eleanor Updegraff who first suggested the perfect title; Tom Clohosy Cole who's made *The Climbers*, *The Den* and now *The List* so glorious to spot on the shelves; Catherine Coe for her care and expertise; Ailsa Bathgate and the whole Barrington Stoke team who truly are second-to-none.

Our books are tested
for children and young people by
children and young people.

Thanks to everyone who consulted on
a manuscript for their time and effort in
helping us to make our books better
for our readers.